DISCARD

D0393710

Presented to

Helen Hall Library

By

The Houston Area Library

System through a grant from

the Texas State Library

APR 0 7

WEIRD STORIES
FROM THE
Lonesome Café

JUDY COX

WEIRD STORIES
FROM THE
Lonesome Café

Illustrated by
Diane Kidd

Harcourt, Inc.

San Diego   New York   London

Text copyright © 2000 by Judy Cox
Illustrations copyright © 2000 by Diane Kidd

All rights reserved. No part of this publication may be reproduced
or transmitted in any form or by any means, electronic or mechanical,
including photocopy, recording, or any information storage and retrieval
system, without permission in writing from the publisher.

Requests for permission to make copies of any part of the work should be
mailed to the following address: Permissions Department, Harcourt, Inc.,
6277 Sea Harbor Drive, Orlando, Florida 32887-6777.

Library of Congress Cataloging-in-Publication Data
Cox, Judy.
Weird stories from the Lonesome Café/Judy Cox; illustrated by Diane Kidd.
p.   cm.
Summary: Sam moves to Nevada with his uncle to run a café in the middle
of nowhere, and although Uncle Clem insists that nothing ever happens
there, his clientele consists of a number of strange characters, including
Dorothy and Toto, Elvis, and Bigfoot.
[1. Restaurants—Fiction.   2. Uncles—Fiction.   3. Nevada—Fiction.
4. Humorous stories.] I. Kidd, Diane, ill. II. Title.
PZ7.C83835We   2000
[Fic]—dc21   98-56016
ISBN 0-15-202134-5

K J I H G F E

Printed in China

The illustrations in this book were done in Higgins drawing ink
on Canson acid-free watercolor paper, cold press surface.
The display type was set in Litterbox.
The text type was set in Berkeley Old Style Medium.
Printed by South China Printing Company, Ltd., China
This book was printed on 128 gsm Japanese matte paper.
Production supervision by Stanley Redfern and Pascha Gerlinger
Designed by Linda Lockowitz

To Tim and Tiffer,
who provide my daily quota of silliness,
and to Linda Z.,
who stuck with the story.
—J. C.

To Linda Z., Marylou M., Deborah H., Linda L., and
Cheryl H. for your wisdom and kindness.
And to my friends and family,
especially Bobby and Alex, for your love and support,
which included letting me cover the
living room wall with artwork.
—D. K.

Contents

CHAPTER ONE

The Lonesome Café

NOTHING ever happens here," said Uncle Clem. He wadded up another piece of paper and threw it at the wastebasket. It bounced off the rim and fell on the floor with the others.

I've tried to tell him. But he won't listen. He's wrong. Things *do* happen in this café. Weird things. Amazing things.

Uncle Clem's an author. At least, that's what he's going to be...soon as he writes his book.

Last month Uncle Clem bought this

place out West. I call it the Lonesome Café. Nothing but jackrabbits and coyotes. And quiet. Plenty of quiet.

At least, that's what I thought at first.

"I need peace and quiet, Sam," Uncle Clem told me last month as we packed to move. I've lived with Uncle Clem since January. My parents are biologists. I live with Uncle Clem whenever they're out of the country. This year they're studying harpy eagles in Venezuela. I miss my parents; but it's fun to be with Uncle Clem.

I crammed my old copies of *Weird and Amazing Tales* on top of my baseball glove. I closed the box and taped it shut.

"City life—you can have it!" continued Uncle Clem. He shoved the box into the car with the others. The backseat was so full of boxes you couldn't see out the windows.

He hooked a bungee cord around the

trunk to hold it closed. "Noise, noise, noise! Car horns, boom boxes, trains, boats, planes! Nevada will be peaceful after this. Think of it, boy. Fresh air! Starry nights! Wide-open spaces! I'm sure to get my book done out there." School wouldn't start for two more months, so I'd have the rest of the summer to help out.

I liked the looks of the café right from the start. It was the only building for miles and miles. One big old cottonwood tree gave a bit of shade.

Inside was cozy. There were four tables with chairs, for customers. Along one side ran a wide counter with a pass-through to the kitchen. Six stools were pulled up to the counter. Across the room from the counter was a row of windows.

While I worked I could look outside and see the desert. Brown rocks and bare blue mountains rose up to the sky. Lots of sky.

I wiped the counter. Uncle Clem baked

some pies and swept the floor. I made a
sign. He hung it on the front door.

We were open for business.

Tires squealed. I looked outside. Dust
and more dust. A tumble of tumbleweeds.
The dust cleared and I saw a van. The sign
on the side read CHANNEL 54 NEWS. Great!
Our first customers!

I grabbed the menus. Uncle Clem put
on the coffeepot.

"Howdy!" Uncle Clem said. "Make
yourselves to home." Uncle Clem talks like
that. He's from Oklahoma.

They sat at the counter. A skinny woman
with long red fingernails, a tall man with a

hat, and a short man with a dark bristly mustache.

"Cup of joe," said the woman.

"Me, too," said the short man.

"Make that three," said the tall man.

Uncle Clem poured three coffees, black.

"How about some pie?" I asked.

"Make mine apple," said the news-woman.

"I'll have a burger," said the tall man. "And a side of fries."

"And a bowl of chili with extra onion rings," said the short man.

I slid Uncle Clem a look. He made great pies, but chili? Fries? Extra onion rings? I didn't know if we were up to it.

"Yes siree, folks!" Uncle Clem said. "Eve with the lid on, burger, fries, rings, and a bowl of red! Coming right up!"

Uncle Clem had taught me diner slang, so I knew what he meant. "Eve with the lid on" is apple pie—because of Adam and

Eve, and the apple. A "bowl of red" is a bowl of chili. A "cup of joe" is a cup of coffee.

I ran around back, to the grill. I tied on an apron and plopped a tall white hat onto my head. I dropped a frozen hamburger patty onto the grill. It sizzled.

Uncle Clem turned the stove up to heat the chili.

Black smoke curled up from the burger. *Uh-oh, the grill must be too hot!* I raced to flip the burger over.

Sizz! Streams of chili bubbled down the sides of the pot. I ran to turn the stove down.

Zeeeeppp! The burning burger set off the smoke detector! Uncle Clem grabbed a stool and climbed up to turn it off.

He lost his balance and teetered, falling onto a stack of clean pans. *Crash!* The pans tumbled down, bouncing and skidding into the swinging door. *Bam! Bang! Bash!*

I helped Uncle Clem up. He rubbed his elbow.

"What's taking so long?" called the newswoman. "We're in a hurry here! Off to catch a news story!"

"Yeah," said the tall man. "Where are my fries?"

While Uncle Clem turned off the chili, I flipped the burger onto a plate. Or at least that's what I tried to do.

"Nice catch," said Uncle Clem.

I slathered on lots of ketchup so the tall man wouldn't taste the burned parts. Uncle Clem put a slice of apple pie onto a plate. He ladled chili into a bowl. A tad sloshed over the side. I hoped no one would notice.

I threw some fries and rings onto a clean plate, and took off my hat and apron. Then I ran around to the counter. Uncle Clem slid the plates across the pass-through.

I set the plates in front of the diners. The newswoman looked at her pie. She looked at me. Her eyes narrowed. I held my breath.

She took a bite. "Mmm," she said. I sighed with relief.

After they left, Uncle Clem and I surveyed the mess. I sank down onto the floor, exhausted just from looking: Dirty plates stacked up. Greasy pots overflowing the sink. The floor so covered with crumbs, it crunched when I walked.

"Won't get any writing done today." Uncle Clem sighed.

I tied my apron back on and began to sweep.

The next day, we hung a new sign on the door:

CHAPTER TWO

Harry

AFTER the *Channel 54 News* team left, things got very quiet. Too quiet. In fact, we hadn't had a customer in a week.

If this kept up, Uncle Clem would never have anything to write about!

So when this guy walked in, I was glad to see him.

"Sit yourself down, young feller!" Uncle Clem said. I wiped off a stool.

"You look a mite hungry." Uncle Clem handed him a menu. "How 'bout a nice BLT?"

The fellow nodded. His long hair shook up and down. I've never seen anyone with that much hair. It looked like a lion's mane.

And tall, oh yes! He was tall! Must have been seven, eight feet.

And speaking of feet—no wonder he didn't have shoes. His feet were bigger than a pro basketball player's!

Uncle Clem fixed him a couple BLTs, extra mayo. And a side of fries.

Four of them.

And a pot of coffee. Black. And some lemon cream pie.

A whole one.

The big guy ate like he hadn't seen food in quite a while. I polished a spot on the counter with my apron.

"Down on your luck?" Uncle Clem asked.

The big guy nodded.

"Hard times?" Uncle Clem said.

The big guy sighed. His eyes looked sad.

Just then, tires squealed outside. I looked out the window. A van pulled up in a big cloud of dust and braked to a stop.

CHANNEL 54 NEWS was painted on the side.

The hairy man looked scared. He slipped behind the counter and into the kitchen. Big as he was, it wasn't easy. Now, what was he up to? Before I could follow him, the news team came in. They sat down at the counter.

"Three cups of joe, coming up!" Uncle Clem said. I ran to get cups and saucers for coffee.

"We're looking for Bigfoot," said the

newswoman. She pointed to the magazine she carried.

I took it. The latest issue of *Weird and Amazing Tales*. I didn't have this one yet. I looked at the cover. LEGENDARY MISSING LINK BETWEEN MAN AND BEAST! read the headline. The picture was blurry. I looked closer.

It was the hairy man in the kitchen!

I tried to show Uncle Clem, but the newswoman grabbed it back. "Bigfoot's a myth," Uncle Clem said. "No such animal."

The newswoman tapped the magazine with a long red fingernail. "It says here that Bigfoot's been spotted in your area." She looked at me.

"Uncle Clem," I whispered. "I need to talk to you. Right now!"

But Uncle Clem was busy refilling the coffee cups. And the newswoman was staring at me as if she could drill holes into my brain.

I thought about the big guy in back. His sad eyes. How hungry he'd been. I swallowed.

The short man narrowed his eyes. "It's worth a lot of money if you can tell us where to find him," he said.

"Sorry," Uncle Clem said. "Nothing ever happens here." He handed out menus. "Now, how about a nice slice of lemon pie?"

Crash! Sounded like a whole pile of pans falling down in the kitchen. Uncle Clem and the *Channel 54 News* team ran back to see. But I got there first.

I couldn't believe it. It was the long-haired fellow! His hair was tied in a pony-tail now, and he was wearing an apron and a tall white hat. He was frying up some burgers.

The newswoman looked him up and down. She craned her neck. Her eyes narrowed. "Say!" she said. "Aren't you—?"

The hairy fellow flipped the burgers into the air. They turned upside down and landed on the grill. I watched in admiration. Right side up. Not one speck burned.

The newswoman stopped talking. She sniffed. "Mmm," she said. "Make me a couple of those."

"Me, too!" said the tall man.

"I'll take mine with extra onions," added the man with the bristly mustache.

"Extra onions coming right up!" I said.

The *Channel 54 News* team sat down again. They all ate burgers and fries.

When they finished eating, the newswoman paid the tab. She looked at Uncle Clem. She looked at me. "We'll be back," she said. "My nose for news tells me there's a story here, somewhere. And I'm never wrong."

"He was too tall for Bigfoot, anyway," she told her news team as they walked out the door.

"Probably plays for the Lakers," said the man with the mustache.

I watched them drive away.

Back in the kitchen, the big guy, Uncle Clem, and I washed up. "Harry," Uncle Clem said to the big guy, "we don't get many customers out here. Not much excitement. In fact, nothing ever happens. But if it's quiet you're looking for, this is the place."

Harry seemed to like his new name. He nodded.

That's how we got our short-order cook.

CHAPTER THREE

EL

HARRY settled right in. Uncle Clem taught him to make a lemon pie and a mean cup of joe. I was relieved. Now Uncle Clem would have time to write. He'd surely get his book done.

But business was picking up, and we had to drive to Vegas for hamburger buns. Two hundred miles, round-trip. Making that trip three times a week sure cut into Uncle Clem's writing time!

I was putting the bread away one afternoon, when the door jangled. I'd hung a little bunch of bells above the door. They rang when somebody walked in. Like now.

I went out to greet our customer. He looked sort of familiar.

Uncle Clem must have thought so, too. "You from around these parts, mister?" he asked.

The fellow shook his head. His dark hair was slicked back and waved up high.

"Don't get too many strangers here," Uncle Clem said. I looked out the window. A pink 1950s Cadillac was parked in the lot. A pink Caddy! Now where had I read about one of those? I dug the latest issue of *Weird and Amazing Tales* out from under the counter.

The man sat down.

"What can I get you?" Uncle Clem asked, handing him a menu.

"Sandwich," said the stranger. "Make it peanut butter, fried banana, and bacon. And a double chocolate malt, please."

Uncle Clem called the order back to Harry, while I thumbed through my magazine. A few minutes later, Harry slid the plate across the pass-through. I set the plate on the counter, in front of the dark-haired fellow.

"Thank you," drawled the man. "Thank you very much."

When he finished eating, he went over to the jukebox. It was Uncle Clem's pride and joy. A vintage 'box from 1958.

"Don't make them like that anymore," Uncle Clem said to the man.

"No sir," said the stranger. "She's a beaut. Like to hear something?"

He put in a nickel and punched some numbers. The sound of twangy guitars filled the café. Old rock 'n' roll.

"My kind of music," said Uncle Clem. He tapped his foot.

The man at the counter knew all the words. He sang along softly and tapped his

foot, too. He had on a strange pair of shoes. Blue suede.

I found the page in *Weird and Amazing Tales*. "Uncle Clem," I whispered. "I need to talk to you. Right now!"

But before Uncle Clem could answer, tires squealed outside. I looked out the window. Wouldn't you know! The *Channel 54 News* van skidded up in a cloud of dust.

Uncle Clem put on a pot of joe.

"Get out the pie!" I hollered to Harry.

Uncle Clem opened the door. "Come on in, folks," he said. He poured the coffee.

"We've had reports Elvis was sighted

around here," said the newswoman as they sat down.

The music stopped. The stranger at the counter put on his sunglasses. He pulled the collar of his jacket up high. He picked up a menu and held it up close to his face.

The short man narrowed his eyes. "It's worth a lot of money if you can tell us where to find him," he said.

Uncle Clem shook his head. "Elvis, the king of rock and roll?" he said. "Sorry to disappoint you folks, but Elvis has been dead since '77."

The newswoman looked at the man with the dark hair. Her eyes narrowed. "You there!" she called. She walked over. She looked him up and down, tapping her long fingernails against her folded arms. "Do you play guitar?" she demanded. "Sing?"

"No ma'am," he said. "I'm just..." He paused and looked at me.

Something about his eyes reminded me

of Harry. I folded *Weird and Amazing Tales* closed and slid it under the counter. "Delivering bread!" I said quickly, then held my breath. Would they buy it?

"Bread delivery? Hot diggety!" said Uncle Clem. "Just what I need to give me more time to write. Say, how 'bout putting me on your route?" he added. "I could use a double order of hamburger buns, and some sliced white bread."

"Sure thing, little buddy," said the stranger with the pink Cadillac.

The newswoman narrowed her eyes. She stared at the stranger. She stared at me. Finally she shrugged. "All right," she said. "But we'll be back. My nose for news tells me there's a story here, somewhere."

They started to leave. The tall man shook his head. "Anyway, he can't be Elvis," he pointed out. "Elvis was fat. This man is thin."

"Elvis wasn't fat when he was young,"

argued the man with the bristly mustache.

"No, no, you're right. But this man is *too* thin," said the tall man.

"Elvis is dead," said Uncle Clem, shaking his head.

But the *Channel 54 News* team had driven away.

After the van disappeared in a cloud of dust, the stranger looked at me. "Just call me El," he said. He paid his bill and left.

I began to clear up. Under El's plate was a tip. But what a tip! A hundred-dollar bill!

"Uncle Clem!" I said. "Look at this!" But Uncle Clem was lost in thought. He was sitting at a table in back, staring at a blank piece of paper.

I shook my head and slipped the hundred-dollar bill into the cash register. Weird.

CHAPTER FOUR

Mr. C

THE NEXT DAY I had a phone call from Mom and Dad. Mom said their work was going well and they might be back by Christmas. Great!

I looked outside. The man with the blue suede shoes was back. He opened the trunk of his pink Cadillac and began to unload the bread we'd ordered. I don't know how he got all that bread in the trunk of his Caddy, but I sure was glad to see him.

A couple of days later, Uncle Clem took the hundred-dollar tip and bought a type-writer. He set up a table at the back of the café. He had his typewriter and a fresh stack of clean white paper. He had a pile of sharpened pencils. He had a pink eraser. He looked ready to roll.

"You're all set now, Uncle Clem," I said, filling the saltshakers.

Uncle Clem bit his pencil and sighed. "Only one problem," he said. "No stories. In the city, lots of things happened. Lots to write about. Out here . . . " He sighed. He stared out the window. The jackrabbits stared back.

"But Uncle Clem!" I said. "What about Harry? What about El? Couldn't you write about them?"

"A short-order cook and a bread delivery-man?" He chuckled, and patted me on the head. "Wouldn't be much of an exciting book, would it?"

He typed a sentence. But then he yanked out the paper, wadded it up, and threw it into the wastebasket. With all the other wadded-up pieces of paper. "If only something would happen." He sighed.

Just then something did happen. But not the kind of thing you'd want to write about. *Fizzz!* That leaky old pipe under the kitchen sink burst again.

Uncle Clem pushed his chair back. I ran to get the toolbox.

Harry was in the kitchen, mopping frantically. Water squirted out all over the place from the leaky pipe. The faster he mopped, the faster it squirted. Uncle Clem climbed under the sink. The bells on the door jangled. I ran to greet our customer.

A man sat down at the counter. He had a full white beard. Red cheeks, red nose. A tad overweight.

I got out the senior-citizen menu.

"Nice place you got here," he said. He put on a pair of little gold-rimmed glasses.

"Thanks," I said. "We like it." I polished the counter with a corner of my apron.

"The vanilla shake sounds good," he said. Harry stopped mopping and made a shake. He whipped it right out, and I set it in front of the old fellow. He looked out the window while he drank.

I looked, too. His rig was parked in the lot. Red station wagon. White trailer, green trim. Dusty.

"Been driving long?" I asked.

He nodded. "From up North." He seemed to be itching to talk.

"Just finished my busiest season ever," he said. "So this year I decided to take a vacation. Drove till I found someplace warm. No reindeer, no helpers, no snow. Nothing but quiet."

Reindeer! Just how far north did he come from? "We got quiet," I said. I looked at him a little closer. Red cheeks: check. White beard: check. Round little belly: check. No. It couldn't be!

Fizzz!

"*Help!*" yelled Uncle Clem.

That doggone leaky pipe must have burst again. I dashed into the kitchen. This time water shot up like Old Faithful. It hit the ceiling and splashed everywhere. Uncle Clem danced up and down in frustration. Harry held his white chef's hat over the pipe, but the water just kept coming.

"Where's the shut-off valve?" called the customer. He'd followed me into the kitchen.

"Out back!" I yelled over the noise of the water and Harry's howls.

In a minute the geyser turned into a cascade, then a trickle, then stopped entirely. The ceiling dripped. The walls dripped. The floor sloshed. Water streamed down Harry's face, hair, and clothes. Uncle Clem looked mad as a wet hen. I wrung out my apron.

"Got a wrench?" asked the old gent when he came back inside.

Without a word I handed him the toolbox. He rummaged around for a minute and then disappeared under the sink. Couple of minutes later, out he popped. "That's the ticket," he said. "Let's try her now."

Harry, Uncle Clem, and I watched anxiously as the fellow went out back to turn the water on. I held my breath. No leaks.

The old guy came back in and turned the faucet. Water rushed out and down the drain, tame as you please.

"Say, where'd you learn how to fix things?" Uncle Clem asked.

The old gent smiled. "I've got a pretty big workshop up North. Even have my own delivery service."

"Why don't you park your rig here?"

Uncle Clem said. "I could use a good handyman."

"It's a deal!" The old gent laughed. His belly shook. "Just call me Mr. C," he added. "Ho, ho, ho." He laid his finger beside his nose and winked at me.

CHAPTER FIVE

Dot

WITH HARRY, Mr. C, and El helping out, I just knew Uncle Clem would get his book started.

He was sitting in front of the typewriter, trying to think, when a dust devil blew up outside.

A big one. It looked like a little tornado. It swirled around, whipping up dust, jack-rabbits, and tumbleweeds, then spun out of sight.

A few minutes later the bells jangled. The door opened and a girl walked in.

She had a little dog with her. She looked around at the jukebox, the lunch counter, the stools.

I knew I'd seen her somewhere before.

"I don't think we're in Kansas anymore," she said to her dog.

"Nope," I said. "You're in Nevada."

Uncle Clem came over. "Sit yourself down," he said. "You look like you could use one of my special chocolate malts."

She sat at the counter.

"Far from home?" Uncle Clem asked, handing her the chocolate malt. The girl nodded sadly.

"There's no place like home," she said with a sigh. She took a sip.

I looked outside. Strange weather. First a dust devil, and now clouds. Funny-shaped clouds. Almost looked like they spelled something.

"'Surrender Dorothy,'" I read. I looked at the girl.

Surrender Dorothy

She turned pale. "Call me Dot," she said. "Uncle Henry does."

"How about something for your little dog, too?" Uncle Clem asked.

"That's Toto," she said. The dog barked.

I handed Dot a bowl of water.

Just then we heard a holler from Harry, in the kitchen. I ran back to see. Uncle Clem and the girl were close on my heels.

A dish towel next to the stove had caught fire and fallen to the floor. Flames curled up.

"Stand back!" yelled Dot. She flung the water in Toto's dish onto the burning towel.

47

Sizz! The fire sputtered out slowly. A cloud of smoke rolled up.

"Quick thinking," said Uncle Clem.

"Doesn't it look like it's . . . melting?" Dot asked.

I looked at her standing there holding the empty water dish, her little dog right beside her. Now I knew where I'd seen her!

"Uncle Clem!" I said. "I need to talk to you right away!"

But before I could tell him, there was a squeal of tires out front.

The *Channel 54 News* team pulled up in a cloud of dust. Uncle Clem put on a pot of joe. I got out the pie.

The news team sat at the counter. Uncle Clem poured the coffee.

"We're looking for a witch," said the newswoman. She looked at Dot.

Uncle Clem shook his head. "Witches are a myth. No such animal."

The newswoman pointed a red-tipped finger at the fading skywriting outside. "What about that?" she said.

Uncle Clem shrugged. "Funny weather," he said.

The short man narrowed his eyes. "It's worth a lot of money if you can tell us where to find the witch," he said.

The newswoman looked at Dot. "Don't I know you from somewhere?"

"Oh, no ma'am," she said. Her eyes looked scared. She turned to me. "I'm... I'm..."

"The new waitress!" I said quickly. She smiled.

"The new waitress!" Uncle Clem said.

"Hot diggety! Now I'll have more time to write!"

The short man bent to pet the dog. The little dog growled. The man quickly pulled his hand back.

The newswoman stared at Dot. She stared at me. She stared at Dot's little dog, too.

Finally she shrugged. "OK," she said. "But we'll be back. My nose for news tells me there's a story here, somewhere. I know we'll find it soon."

"Anyway, she can't be a witch," the short man said. "Witches don't have dogs. Witches have cats. Black cats."

"He's right," agreed the tall man as they walked out the door. "Black *cats,* not black *dogs.*"

"Witches aren't real," said Uncle Clem.

The *Channel 54 News* team drove away.

"Looking for witches." Uncle Clem shook his head. "Good luck to them.

When are they going to learn that nothing ever happens out here?" He settled back down at his typewriter.

I gave Dot an apron and told her about our lunch specials.

"Look," she said, pointing out the window. "There's a rainbow!"

CHAPTER SIX

The Wreck

WITH HARRY in the kitchen, Dot waiting tables, El delivering bread, and Mr. C fixing things, Uncle Clem's days were free to write.

"Only thing, Sam," he told me, "still nothing to write about. If only something interesting would happen!"

"But Uncle Clem," I said. "What about Mr. C? What about Dot?"

He roughed up my hair. "It's clear you're too young to know what makes a good book." He chuckled. "You'd understand if you were a writer. Can't write a best-seller about a handyman and a wait-ress."

I shook my head in disbelief.

El came with the bread. I got him today's menu.

The mailman came in. Great! He gave me a letter from Mom and Dad and my new magazine. I put the letter in my pocket to read later and picked up *Weird and Amazing Tales*. The cover showed an alien and a spaceship. I couldn't wait to read it. I slid it under the counter until after the lunch rush.

Mr. C came in for lunch. Dot poured him a cup of joe. Harry rattled pots in back.

Uncle Clem and I went into the kitchen to wash the breakfast dishes. The stack of dirty dishes towered up to the ceiling. Greasy grills, sticky frying pans, scummy dishes, pots of baked-on chili. Ick!

"No time to write today," Uncle Clem said, and sighed.

"I'll do them for you," I offered.

Uncle Clem grinned. "Thanks, Sam. We'll tackle this chore together."

Just then . . .

Crash! A big green flash lit up the sky. We all ran outside. It was some kind of wreck. (Nevada has the worst car wrecks you ever did see. All those lonesome highways, I guess. People get to driving too fast.)

Only thing was, this wreck wasn't on the highway. It was out in the desert.

And it wasn't a car. Or a truck. Or a bus. Or any other thing I'd ever seen the likes of.

Whatever it had been, now it was smoke and twisted metal.

Dot's little dog sniffed at a clump of sagebrush. I went over to see. "Quick, everybody! Someone's hurt!" I called.

I helped him out of the sagebrush. He wasn't badly injured, just scratched.

"Must be all shook up," said El. "He looks a little green."

A *little* green! I've never seen anyone *that* shade.

And speaking of shade, with ears that size, he wouldn't ever need to wear a hat.

And maybe no one else noticed, but I distinctly saw six fingers on each hand. If they were hands.

Uncle Clem, Mr. C, and El lifted the poor guy and carried him into the café.

Dot bandaged his scratches. Harry fixed

him a pattymelt and a cup of joe. By the time his food came, he was feeling better.

He tried to talk. "Can't understand a word he says," said Uncle Clem. "Must be from out of state."

"Out of state! Uncle!" I whispered. "Out of this *world*!"

"Sam," Uncle Clem warned, "be polite, now."

"Must be anxious to get going," said Uncle Clem. He shook his head. "Young feller, that rig of yours, she's pretty beat up. Don't know if we can do much for you."

Just then the *Channel 54 News* van pulled up to the café, tires squealing, dust flying.

Dot wiped the counter. Uncle Clem put on a fresh pot of joe. I got out the menus. In the kitchen Harry fired up the grill. The mouthwatering smell of sizzling burgers floated out.

"We're looking for a UFO," said the newswoman as soon as she opened the door. "We think an alien landed."

I tried not to look at the fellow sitting at the end of the counter.

"No such animal," Uncle Clem said. "UFOs are a myth."

The tall man frowned. "We had a report. A big streak of light. Looked like it came down right about here."

The short man narrowed his eyes. "It's worth a lot of money if you can tell us where to find it," he said.

Uncle Clem shook his head. "See for yourself. Nobody here but us . . . and Dot's little dog, too."

"That's Toto," said Dot.

The newswoman narrowed her eyes. She stared at the new little guy sitting at the end of the counter. "Say," she said, "aren't *you* an—?"

The new guy flinched.

I looked at Harry.

I looked at El.

I looked at Mr. C.

I looked at Dot.

"He's our new dishwasher!" I said quickly.

The new guy nodded and gave me a look. It could have been a smile.

"The new dishwasher? Hot diggety!" Uncle Clem said. "Now I'll surely have time to get my book started!"

But the newswoman wasn't happy. She flung her pencil and notebook to the floor. "That's it for me!" she said. "I quit! This is the last time I come out here on a wild-goose chase!"

"What do you mean?" I asked.

"We thought we'd found Bigfoot—but he turned out to be just a tall cook!

"We thought we'd found Elvis—but he's just a skinny deliveryman!

"We thought we'd found a witch—but she had a dog instead of a cat!

"Now we're after an alien. And guess what? He's a dishwasher! We never find anything. I've had it!"

"Me, too," said the tall man.

"I quit, too," said the man with the mustache. "We can't be a news team in a place where there's no news!"

"Gee, I know how you feel," Uncle Clem said. "It's tough to find stories in a place like this." He smiled at the newswoman. "Say! How 'bout some lunch before you go?"

The new guy tied on an apron and went into the kitchen to start on the dishes.

"We might as well eat," the newswoman

said as Uncle Clem took down the HELP WANTED sign. "Nothing's going to happen here."

"That's right," I said, hiding a grin. "'Cause nothing ever does."

CHAPTER SEVEN

The Ending

BUSINESS was real steady after the *Channel 54 News* team quit. Steady, but ordinary, if you know what I mean.

I had a letter from Mom and Dad saying they'd definitely be back for Christmas. Cool!

Harry, Mr. C, El, Dot, and the new guy worked at the café all summer. One day, while I was refilling the ketchup dispenser, Mr. C came in. He wore a plaid cap and a pair of driving gloves. "Sorry to be leaving, fellows," he told us. "But it's that time of year. Got to head north. My busy season is coming up, you know."

Uncle Clem shook his hand. "You were a great help," he said. "Come back anytime."

Mr. C shook my hand, too. "You've been a real good boy, Sam," he told me. "I won't forget you when the time comes, if you know what I mean." One last chuckle and he was gone, the green and white trailer pulling out and off down the highway, past the tumbleweeds.

Next to go was Dot. One day a big dust devil spun through the parking lot, picking up tumbleweeds, mesquite, jackrabbits, and Dot's little dog, too.

"Toto, wait for me!" she cried. She turned back and gave each of us a great big hug. "I think I'm going to miss you most of all," she said to Harry. She ran into the parking lot. I guess the dust devil picked her up, too, because that was the last we saw of her. I bet she rode it all the way home.

A few days later, El drove up in his pink Caddy. "This is my last bread delivery," he told us, unloading hamburger buns. "Guys like me can't stay in one place too long. I gotta follow that dream." He shook Uncle Clem's hand. The little green dishwasher came out from the kitchen. He untied his apron and left it on the counter.

"You going, too?" I asked, surprised.

"I told the little guy I'd give him a lift," said El. "It's a long, lonely highway. Once he gets to the big city, he's sure to find some of his kin." The two of them got in the Cadillac. "Viva Las Vegas!" El shouted as they drove away. The little green dishwasher waved until they were out of sight.

Only Harry remained. He looked a lot different than when he first came. His long hair was still neatly pulled back in a pony-tail. He wore sandals on his big feet. He never said much, but I thought he looked happier than when he'd first arrived. I hoped he was going to stay for a while.

"School starts tomorrow," I said to Uncle Clem. "I won't have much time to help out, with the long bus ride and home-work and soccer and all. Maybe we better hang up the Help Wanted sign again."

I dusted it off and hung it on the front door. I wondered who would show up next.

The next day, I slid into a seat at my new school.

"Good morning," said Mr. Jensen, the teacher. "I hope you all had a good summer. In fact, that's your first writing assignment." He turned to the chalkboard and wrote the title in big letters: "WHAT I DID ON MY SUMMER VACATION."

Perfect! I picked up my pencil and started to write.

Weird Stories from the Lonesome Café. "'Nothing ever happens here,' said Uncle Clem."

This was going to be fun.